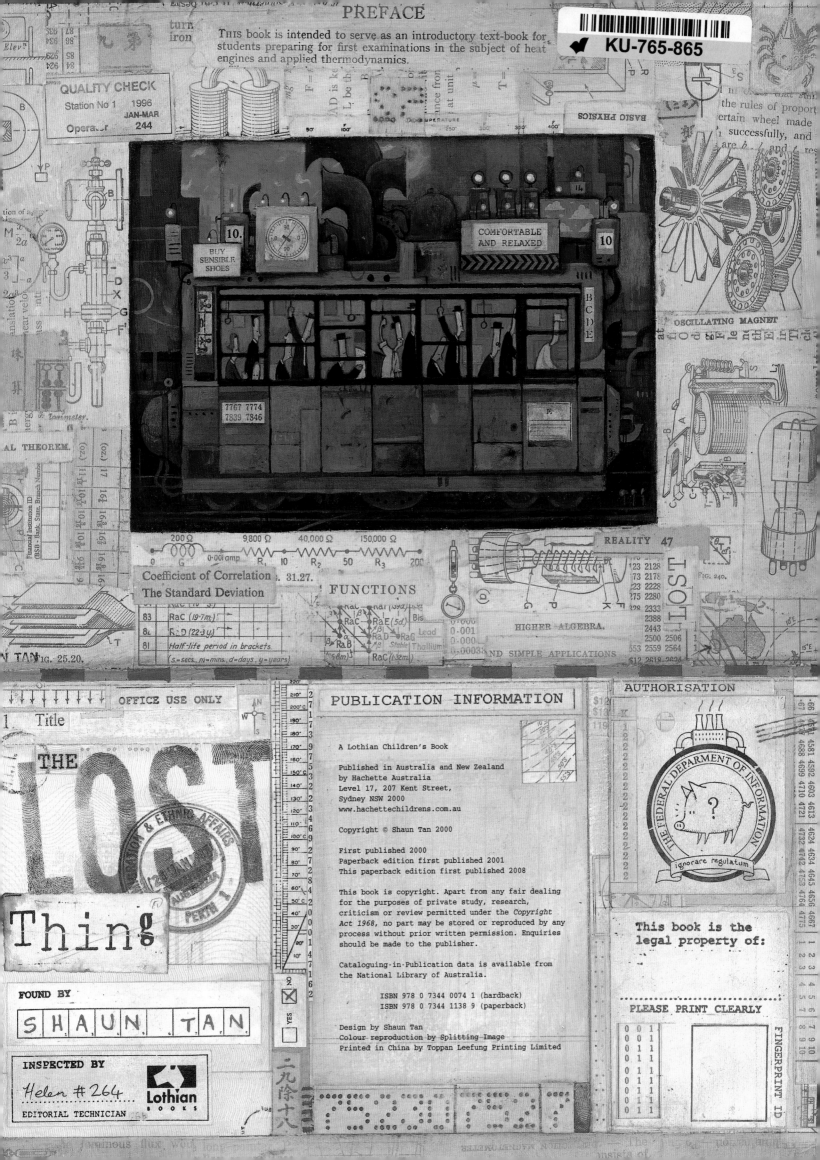

PREFACE

THIS book is intended to serve as an introductory text-book for students preparing for first examinations in the subject of heat engines and applied thermodynamics.

KU-765-865

QUALITY CHECK
Station No 1   1996
JAN-MAR
Operator   244

BUY SENSIBLE SHOES

10.

COMFORTABLE AND RELAXED

10

7767 7774
7839 7846

OSCILLATING MAGNET

REALITY 47

LOST

HIGHER ALGEBRA.

AND SIMPLE APPLICATIONS

Coefficient of Correlation 31.27.
The Standard Deviation

FUNCTIONS

THE **LOST** Thing

FOUND BY
SHAUN TAN

INSPECTED BY
Helen #264
EDITORIAL TECHNICIAN

Lothian BOOKS

PUBLICATION INFORMATION

A Lothian Children's Book

Published in Australia and New Zealand
by Hachette Australia
Level 17, 207 Kent Street,
Sydney NSW 2000
www.hachettechildrens.com.au

Copyright © Shaun Tan 2000

First published 2000
Paperback edition first published 2001
This paperback edition first published 2008

Cataloguing-in-Publication data is available from
the National Library of Australia.

ISBN 978 0 7344 0074 1 (hardback)
ISBN 978 0 7344 1138 9 (paperback)

Design by Shaun Tan
Colour reproduction by Splitting Image
Printed in China by Toppan Leefung Printing Limited

OFFICE USE ONLY

1   Title

AUTHORISATION

THE FEDERAL DEPARTMENT OF INFORMATION

ignorare regulatum

This book is the legal property of:

PLEASE PRINT CLEARLY

FINGERPRINT ID

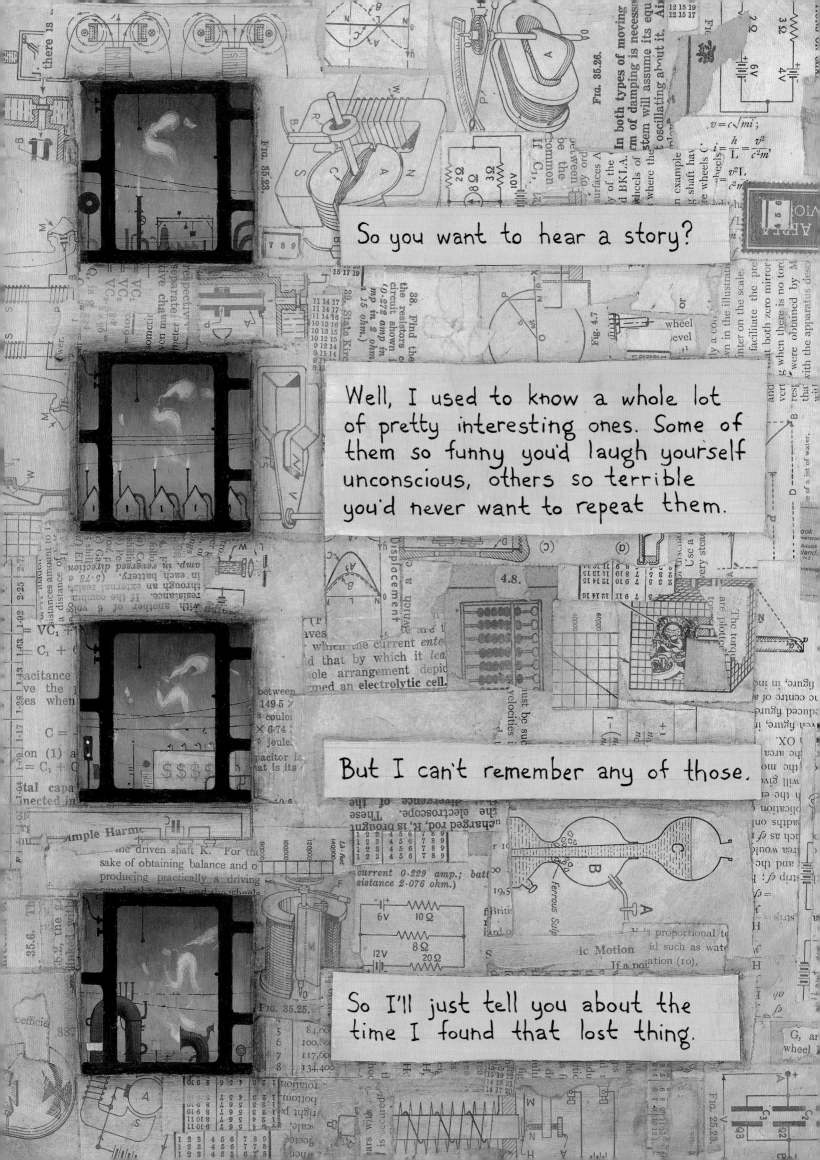

So you want to hear a story?

Well, I used to know a whole lot of pretty interesting ones. Some of them so funny you'd laugh yourself unconscious, others so terrible you'd never want to repeat them.

But I can't remember any of those.

So I'll just tell you about the time I found that lost thing.

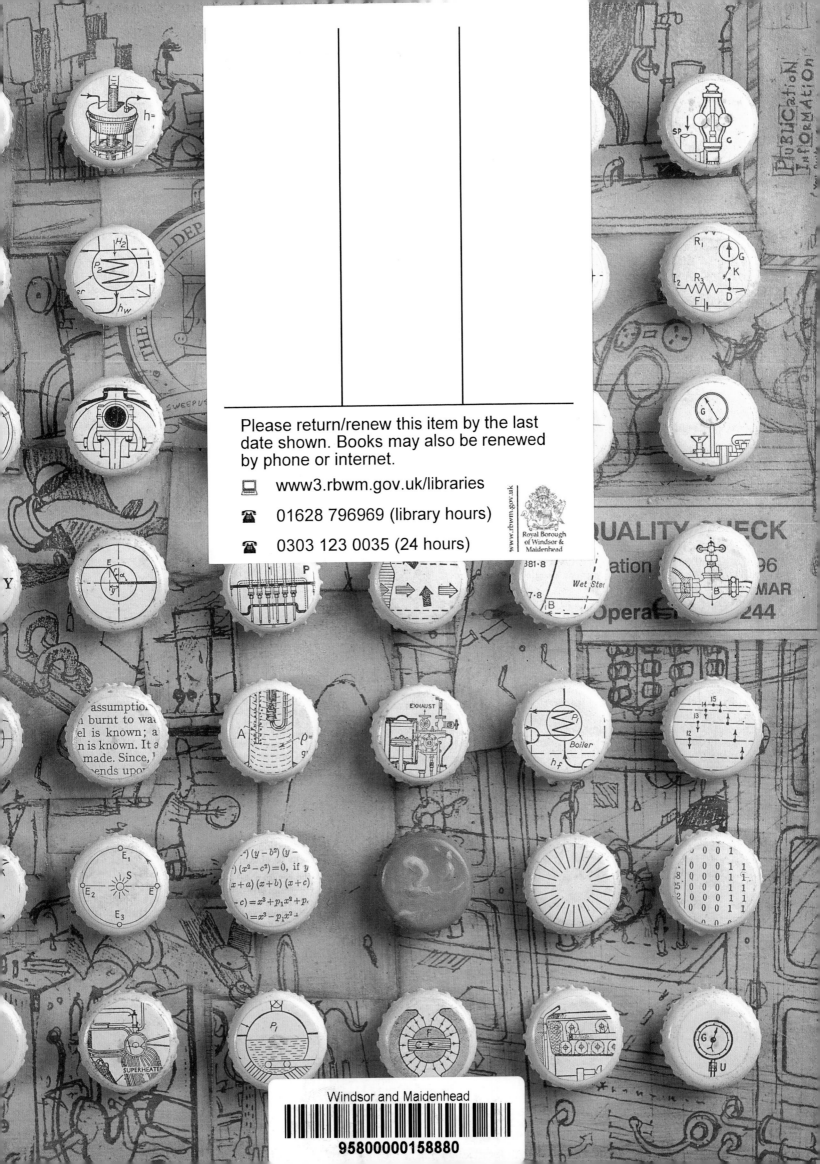

Please return/renew this item by the last date shown. Books may also be renewed by phone or internet.

💻 www3.rbwm.gov.uk/libraries

☎ 01628 796969 (library hours)

☎ 0303 123 0035 (24 hours)

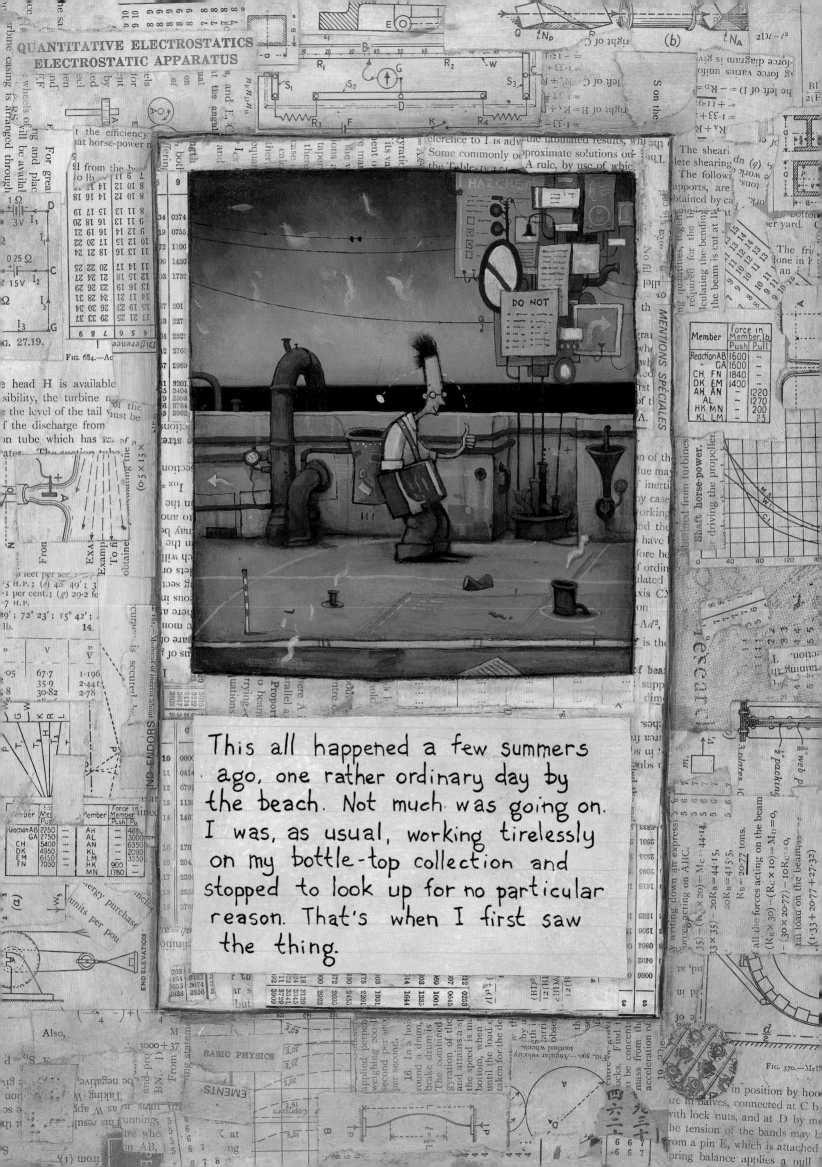

This all happened a few summers ago, one rather ordinary day by the beach. Not much was going on. I was, as usual, working tirelessly on my bottle-top collection and stopped to look up for no particular reason. That's when I first saw the thing.

I must have stared at it for a while. I mean, it had a really weird look about it — a sad, lost sort of look. Nobody else seemed to notice it was there. Too busy doing beach stuff, I guess.

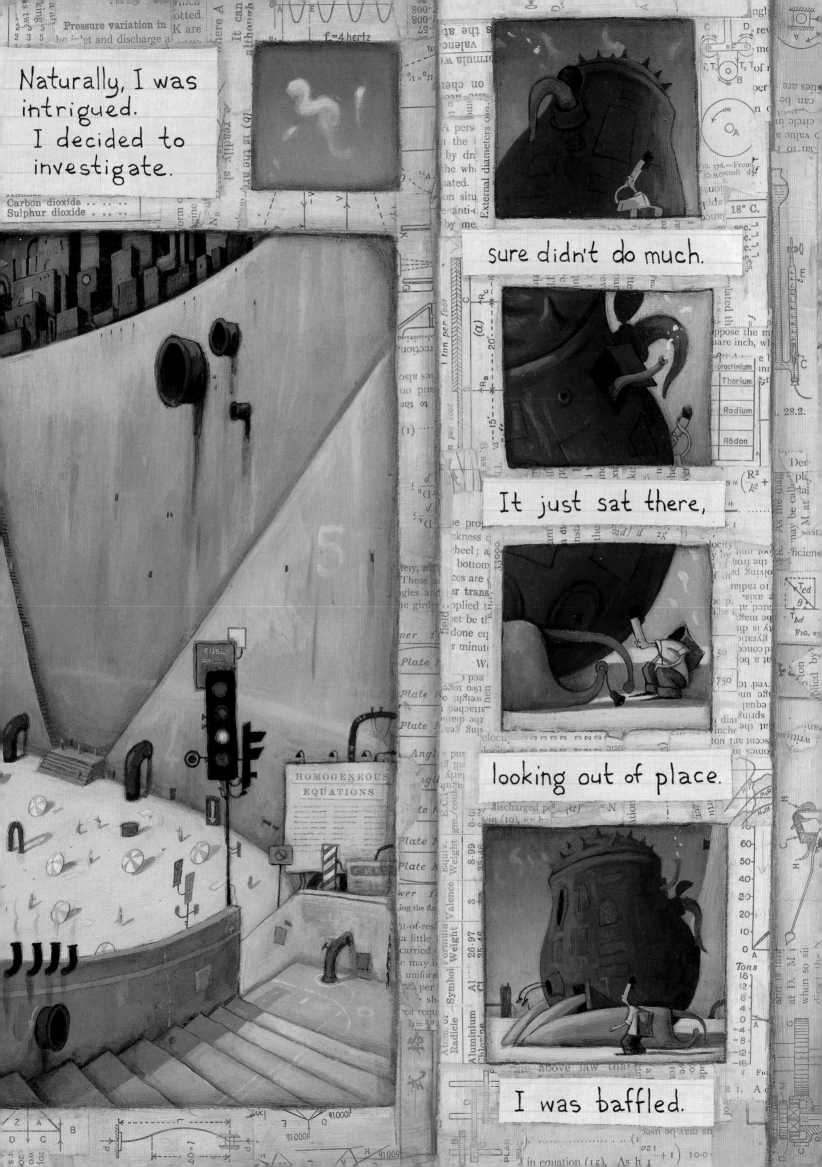

It was quite friendly though, once I started talking to it.

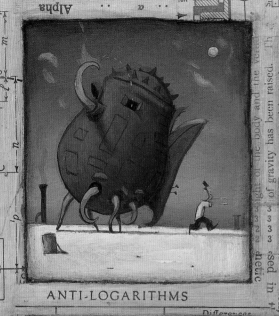

I played with the thing for most of the afternoon. It was great fun, yet I couldn't help feeling that something wasn't quite right.

As the hours slouched by, it seemed less and less likely that anybody was coming to take the thing home. There was no denying the unhappy truth of the situation It was <u>lost</u>.

I asked a few people if they knew anything about it, but nobody was very helpful.

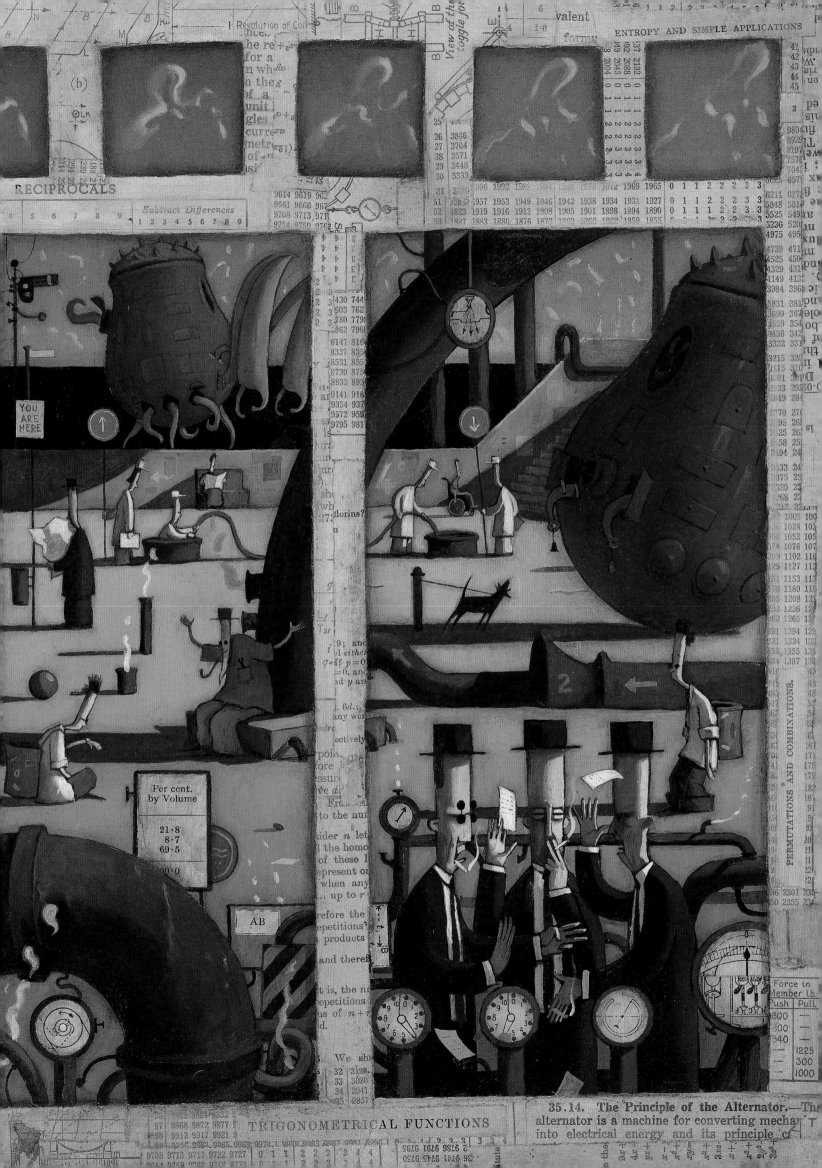

I took the lost thing over to Pete's place. Pete has an opinion on just about everything.

'Cool,' he said.

'I'm trying to find out who owns it,' I told him.
'I dunno, man,' said Pete. 'It's pretty weird. Maybe it doesn't belong to anyone. Maybe it doesn't come from anywhere. Some things are like that...'
He paused for dramatic effect,
'...just plain lost.'

My parents didn't really notice it at first.
Too busy discussing current events, I guess.

Eventually I had to point it out to them.
'Its feet are filthy!' shrieked Mum.
'It could have all kinds of strange diseases,' warned Dad.
'Take it back to where you found it,' they demanded,
both at the same time.
'It's lost,' I said, but they had already started talking
about something else.

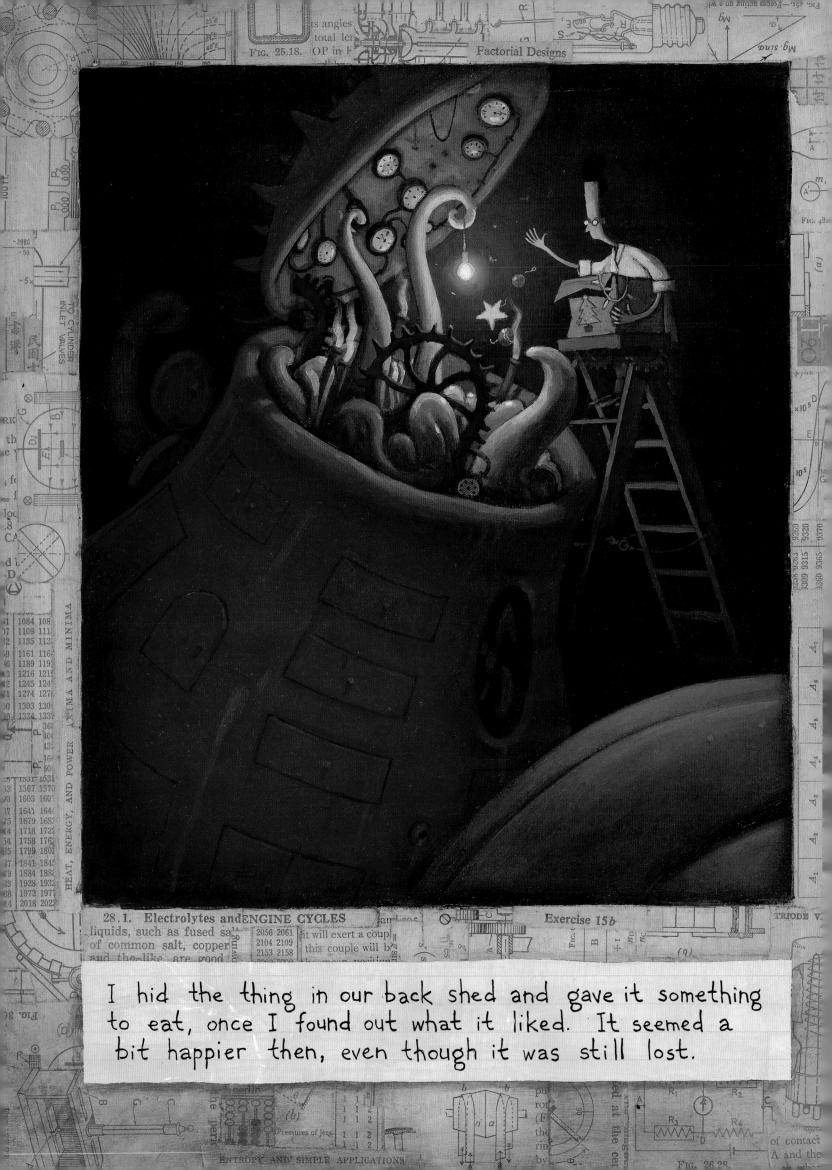

I hid the thing in our back shed and gave it something to eat, once I found out what it liked. It seemed a bit happier then, even though it was still lost.

I checked the local paper for any lost pet notices, but only found a lot of good deals on refrigerator repairs. I remember thinking then that Pete was probably right, that some things were just plain lost. In any case, I sure couldn't keep the thing in the shed forever. Mum or Dad would eventually notice it when they came out looking for a hammer or something.

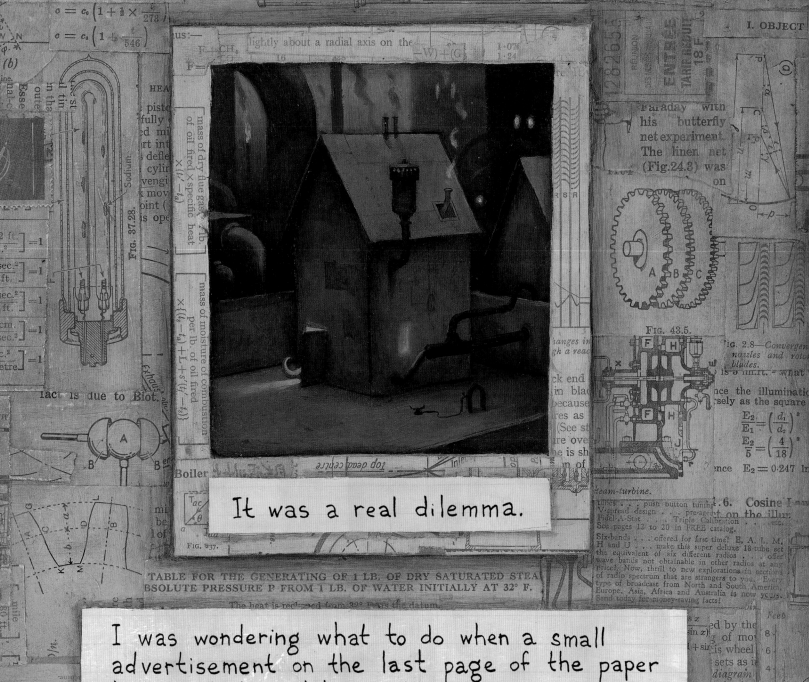

It was a real dilemma.

I was wondering what to do when a small advertisement on the last page of the paper happened to catch my eye.

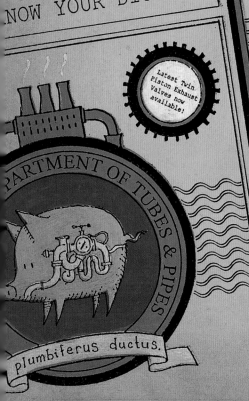

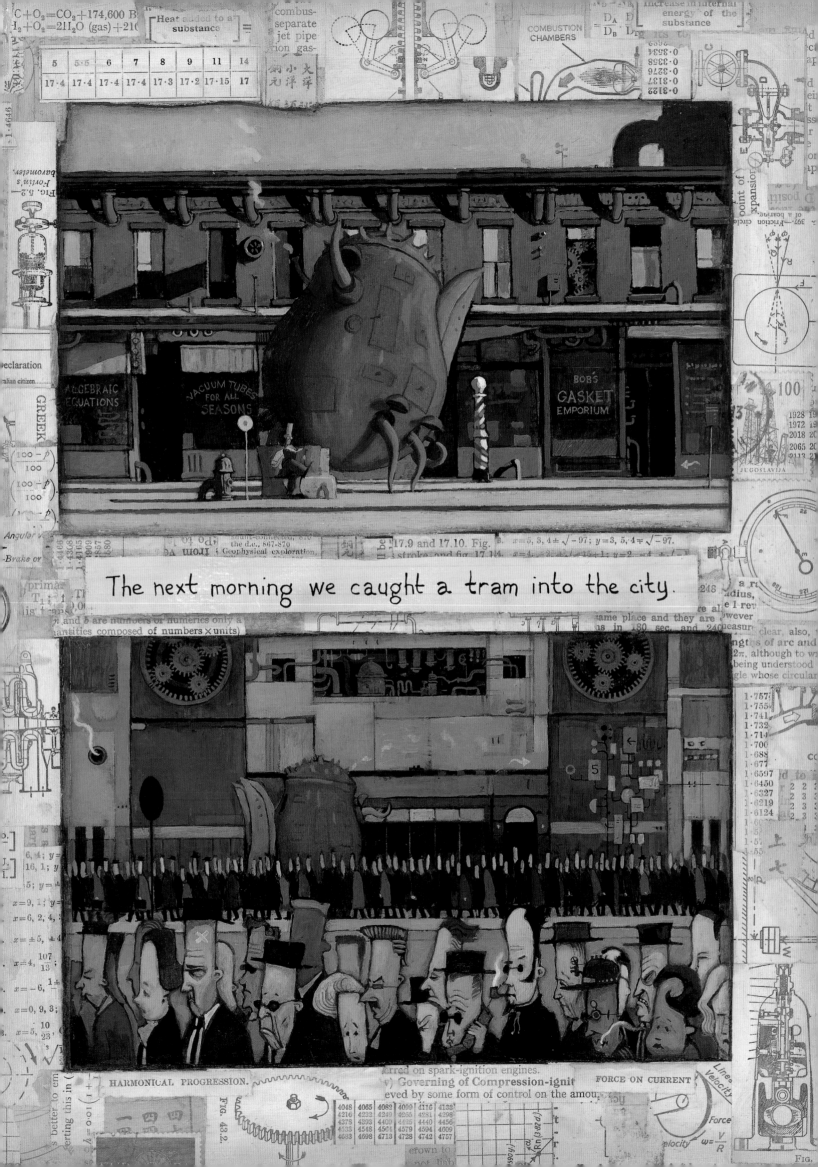

The next morning we caught a tram into the city.

We arrived at a tall grey building with no windows. It was pretty dark in there, and it smelt like disinfectant. 'I have a lost thing,' I called to the receptionist at the front desk.
'Fill in these forms,' she said.

The lost thing made a small, sad noise.

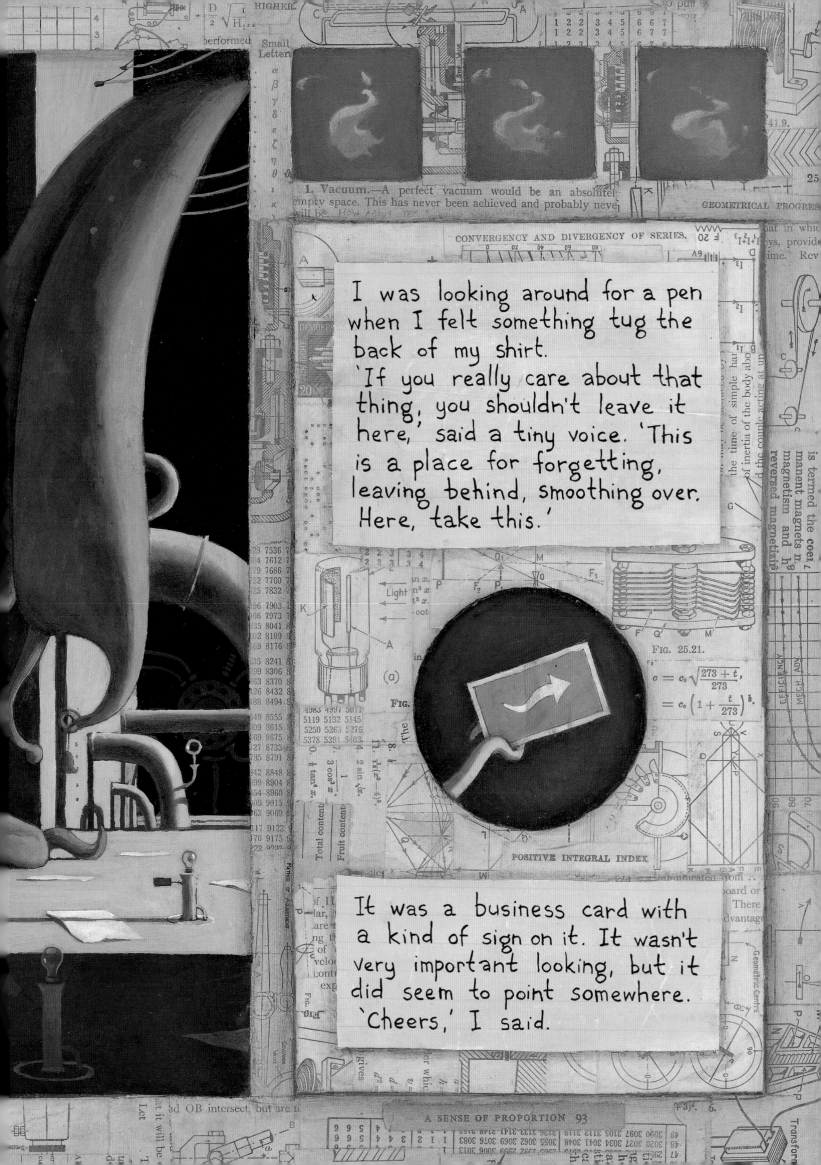

I was looking around for a pen when I felt something tug the back of my shirt.
'If you really care about that thing, you shouldn't leave it here,' said a tiny voice. 'This is a place for forgetting, leaving behind, smoothing over. Here, take this.'

It was a business card with a kind of sign on it. It wasn't very important looking, but it did seem to point somewhere.
'Cheers,' I said.

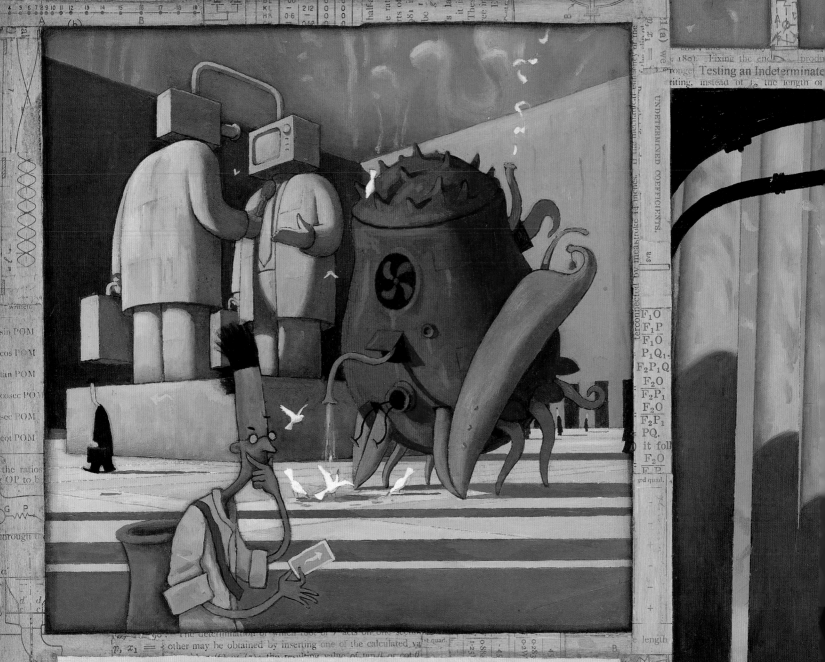

and hunted all over the place for this sign.

It wasn't an easy job,

and I can't say I knew what it all meant.

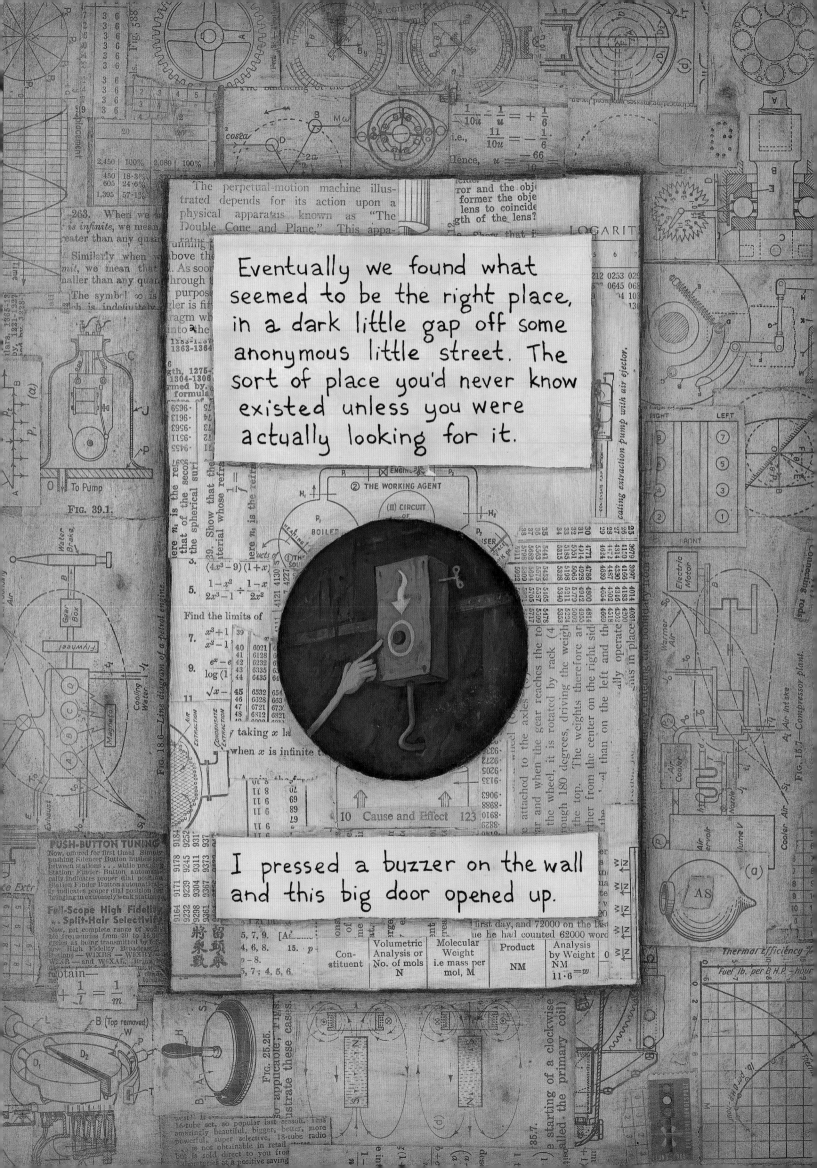

Eventually we found what seemed to be the right place, in a dark little gap off some anonymous little street. The sort of place you'd never know existed unless you were actually looking for it.

I pressed a buzzer on the wall and this big door opened up.

I didn't know what to think, but the lost thing made an approving sort of noise. It seemed as good a time as any to say goodbye to each other. So we did.

Then I went home to classify my bottle-top collection.

Well, that's it. That's the story.
Not especially profound, I know, but I
never said it was.
And don't ask me what the moral is.

I mean, I can't say that the thing
actually belonged in the place where it
ended up. In fact, none of the things
there really belonged. They all seemed
happy enough though, so maybe that
didn't matter. I don't know...

I still think about that lost thing from time to time. Especially when I see something out of the corner of my eye that doesn't quite fit.

You know, something with a weird, sad, lost sort of look.

I see that sort of thing less and less these days though.

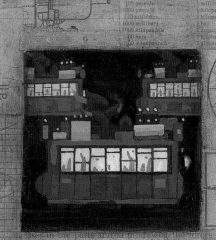

Maybe there aren't many lost things around anymore.

Or maybe I've just stopped noticing them.

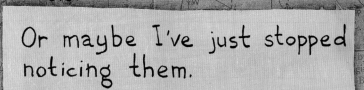

Too busy doing other stuff, I guess.